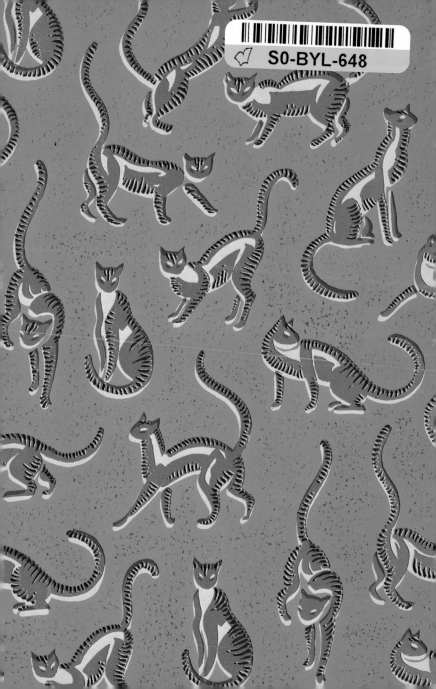

FOR A CAT LOVER

. . . .

. . . .

TOBERMORY

SAKI (H.H.MUNRO)

CLARKSON POTTER/PUBLISHERS

NEW YORK

PUBLISHED BY CLARKSON N. POTTER, INC., 201 EAST 50TH STREET,
NEW YORK, NEW YORK 10022. MEMBER OF THE CROWN PUBLISHING GROUP.

RANDOM HOUSE, INC. NEW YORK, TORONTO, LONDON, SYDNEY, AUCKLAND.

CLARKSON N. POTTER, POTTER, AND COLOPHON
ARE TRADEMARKS OF CLARKSON N. POTTER, INC.

ORIGINALLY PUBLISHED IN GREAT BRITAIN BY
EBURY PRESS LIMITED IN 1994

MANUFACTURED IN HONG KONG
DESIGN BY CARROLL DEMPSEY & THIRKELL LTD
TYPESET BY SX COMPOSING LTD

ISBN 0-517-79981-2

10 9 8 7 6 5 4 3 2 1

FIRST AMERICAN EDITION

TOBERMORY

It was a chill, rain-washed afternoon of a late August day, that indefinite season when partridges are still in security or cold storage, and there is nothing to hunt – unless one is bounded on the north by the Bristol Channel, in which case one may lawfully gallop after fat red stags. Lady Blemley's house-party was not bounded on the north by the Bristol Channel, hence there was a full gathering of her guests round the tea-table on this particular afternoon. And, in spite of the blankness of the season and the triteness of the occasion, there was no trace in the company of that fatigued restlessness which means a dread of the pianola and a subdued hankering for auction bridge. The undisguised open-mouthed attention of the entire party was fixed on the homely negative personality of Mr. Cornelius Appin. Of all her guests, he was the one who had come to Lady Blemley with the vaguest reputation. Some one had said he was 'clever,' and he had got his invitation in the moderate expectation, on the part of his hostess, that some portion at least of his cleverness would be contributed to the general entertainment. Until tea-time that day she had been unable to discover in what direction, if any, his cleverness lay. He was neither a wit nor a croquet champion, a hypnotic force nor a begetter of amateur theatricals. Neither did his exterior suggest the sort of man in whom women are willing to pardon a generous measure of mental deficiency. He had subsided into mere Mr. Appin, and the Cornelius seemed a piece of transparent baptismal bluff. And now he was claiming to have launched on the world a discovery beside which the invention of gunpowder, of the printing-press, and of steam locomotion were inconsiderable trifles. Science had made bewildering strides in many directions during recent decades, but this thing seemed to belong to the domain of miracle rather than to scientific achievement.

'And do you really ask us to believe,' Sir Wilfrid was saying, 'that you have discovered a means for instructing animals in the art of human speech, and that dear old Tobermory has proved your first successful pupil?'

'It is a problem at which I have worked for the last seventeen years,' said Mr. Appin, 'but only during the last eight or nine months have I been rewarded with glimmerings of success. Of course I have experimented with thousands of animals, but latterly only with cats, those wonderful creatures which have assimilated themselves so marvellously with our civilization while retaining all their high-ly developed feral instincts. Here and there among cats one comes across an outstanding superior intellect, just as one does among the ruck of human beings, and when I made the acquaintance of Tobermory a week ago I saw at once that I was in contact with a "Beyond-cat" of extraordinary intelligence. I had gone far along the road to success in recent experiments; with Tobermory, as you call him, I have reached the goal.'

Mr. Appin concluded his remarkable statement in a voice which he strove to divest of a triumphant inflection. No one said 'Rats,' though Clovis's lips moved in a monosyllabic contortion which probably invoked those rodents of disbelief.

'And do you mean to say,' asked Miss Resker, after a slight pause, 'that you have taught Tobermory to say and understand easy sentences of one syllable?'

'My dear Miss Resker,' said the wonder-worker patiently, 'one teaches little children and savages and backward adults in that piece-meal fashion; when one has once solved the problem of making a beginning with an animal of highly developed intelligence one has no need for those halting methods. Tobermory can speak our language with perfect correctness.'

This time Clovis very distinctly said, 'Beyond-rats!' Sir Wilfrid was more polite, but equally sceptical.

'Hadn't we better have the cat in and judge for ourselves?' suggested Lady Blemley.

Sir Wilfrid went in search of the animal, and the company settled themselves down to the languid expectation of witnessing some more or less adroit drawing-room ventriloquism.

In a minute Sir Wilfrid was back in the room, his face white beneath its tan and his eyes dilated with excitement.

'By Gad, it's true!'

His agitation was unmistakably genuine, and his hearers started forward in a thrill of awakened interest.

Collapsing into an armchair he continued breathlessly: 'I found him dozing in the smoking-room, and called out to him to come for his tea. He blinked at me in his usual way, and I said, "Come on, Toby; don't keep us waiting"; and, by Gad! he drawled out in a most horribly natural voice that he'd come when he dashed well pleased! I nearly jumped out of my skin!'

Appin had preached to absolutely incredulous hearers; Sir Wilfrid's statement carried instant conviction. A Babel-like chorus of startled exclamation arose, amid which the scientist sat mutely enjoying the first fruit of his stupendous discovery.

In the midst of the clamour Tobermory entered the room and made his way with velvet tread and studied unconcern across to the group seated round the tea-table.

A sudden hush of awkwardness and constraint fell on the company. Somehow there seemed an element of embarrassment in addressing on equal terms a domestic cat of acknowledged dental ability.

'Will you have some milk, Tobermory?' asked Lady Blemley in a rather strained voice.

'I don't mind if I do,' was the response, couched in a tone of even indifference. A shiver of suppressed excitement went through the listeners, and Lady Blemley might be excused for pouring out the saucer-ful of milk rather unsteadily.

'I'm afraid I've spilt a good deal of it,' she said apologetically.

'After all, it's not my Axminster,' was Tobermory's rejoinder.

Another silence fell on the group, and then Miss Resker, in her best district-visitor manner, asked if the human language had been difficult to learn. Tobermory looked squarely at her for a moment and then fixed his gaze serenely on the middle distance. It was obvious that boring questions lay outside his scheme of life.

'What do you think of human intelligence?' asked Mavis Pellington lamely.

'Of whose intelligence in particular?' asked Tobermory coldly.

'Oh, well, mine for instance,' said Mavis, with a feeble laugh.

'You put me in an embarrassing position,' said Tobermory, whose tone and attitude certainly did not suggest a shred of embarrassment. 'When your inclusion in this house-party was suggested Sir Wilfrid protested that you were the most brainless woman of his acquaintance, and that there was a wide distinction between hospitality and the care of the feeble-minded. Lady Blemley replied that your lack of brain-power was the precise quality which had earned you your invitation, as you were the only person she could think of who might be idiotic enough to buy their old car. You know, the one they call "The Envy of

Sisyphus," because it goes quite nicely up-hill if you push it.'

Lady Blemley's protestations would have had greater effect if she had not casually suggested to Mavis only that morning that the car in question would be just the thing for her down at her Devonshire home.

Major Barfield plunged in heavily to effect a diversion.

'How about your carryings-on with the tortoise-shell puss up at the stables, eh?'

The moment he had said it every one realized the blunder.

'One does not usually discuss these matters in public,' said Tobermory frigidly. 'From a slight observation of your ways since you've been in this house I should imagine you'd find it inconvenient if I were to shift the conversation on to your own little affairs.'

The panic which ensued was not confined to the Major.

'Would you like to go and see if cook has

got your dinner ready?' suggested Lady Blemley hurriedly, affecting to ignore the fact that it wanted at least two hours to Tobermory's dinner-time.

'Thanks,' said Tobermory, 'not quite so soon after my tea. I don't want to die of indigestion.'

'Cats have nine lives, you know,' said Sir Wilfrid heartily.

'Possibly,' answered Tobermory; 'but only one liver.'

'Adelaide!' said Mrs. Cornett, 'do you mean to encourage that cat to go out and gossip about us in the servants' hall?'

The panic had indeed become general. A narrow ornamental balustrade ran in front of most of the bedroom windows at the Towers, and it was recalled with dismay that this had formed a favourite promenade for Tobermory at all hours, whence he could watch the pigeons – and heaven knew what else besides. If he intended to become reminiscent in his present outspoken strain the effect would be something more than disconcerting. Mrs. Cornett, who spent much time at her toilet table, and whose complexion was reputed to be of a nomadic though punctual disposition, looked as ill at ease as the Major. Miss Scrawen, who wrote fiercely sensuous poetry and led a blameless life, merely displayed irritation; if you are methodical and virtuous in private you don't necessarily want every one to know it. Bertie van Tahn, who was so depraved at seventeen that he had long ago given up trying to be any worse, turned a dull shade of gardenia white, but he did not commit the error of dashing out of the room like Odo Finsberry, a young gentleman who was understood to be reading for the Church and who was possibly disturbed at the thought of scandals he might hear concerning other people. Clovis had the presence of mind to maintain a composed exterior; privately he was calculating how long it would take to procure a box of fancy mice through the agency of the *Exchange and Mart* as a species of hush-money.

Even in a delicate situation like the present, Agnes Resker could not endure to remain too long in the background.

'Why did I ever come down here?' she asked dramatically.

Tobermory immediately accepted the opening.

'Judging by what you said to Mrs. Cornett on the croquet-lawn yesterday, you were out for food. You described the Blemleys as the dullest people to stay with that you knew, but said they were clever enough to employ a first-rate cook; otherwise they'd find it difficult to get any one to come down a second time.'

'There's not a word of truth in it! I appeal to Mrs. Cornett – ' exclaimed the discomfited Agnes.

'Mrs. Cornett repeated your remark afterwards to Bertie van Tahn,' continued Tobermory, 'and said, "That woman is a regular Hunger Marcher; she'd go anywhere for four square meals a day," and Bertie van Tahn said – '

At this point the chronicle mercifully ceased. Tobermory had caught a glimpse of the big yellow Tom from the Rectory working his way through the shrubbery towards the stable wing. In a flash he had vanished through the open French window.

With the disappearance of his too brilliant pupil Cornelius Appin found himself beset by a hurricane of bitter upbraiding, anxious inquiry, and frightened entreaty. The responsibility for the situation lay with him, and he must prevent matters from becoming worse. Could Tobermory impart his dangerous gift to other cats? was the first question he had to answer. It was possible, he replied, that he might have initiated his intimate friend the stable puss into his new accomplishment, but it was unlikely that his teaching could have taken a wider range as yet.

'Then,' said Mrs. Cornett, 'Tobermory may be a valuable cat and a great pet; but I'm sure you'll agree, Adelaide, that both he and the stable cat must be done away with without delay.'

'You don't suppose I've enjoyed the last quarter of an hour, do you?' said Lady Blemley bitterly. 'My husband and I are very fond of Tobermory – at least, we were before this horrible accomplishment was infused into him; but now, of course, the only thing is to have him destroyed as soon as possible.'

'We can put some strychnine in the scraps he always gets at dinner-time,' said Sir Wilfrid, 'and I will go and drown the stable cat myself. The coachman will be very sore at losing his pet, but I'll say a very catching form of mange has broken out in both cats and we're afraid of it spreading to the kennels.'

'But my great discovery!' expostulated Mr. Appin; 'after all my years of research and experiment – '

'You can go and experiment on the short-horns at the farm, who are under proper control,' said Mrs. Cornett, 'or the elephants at the Zoological Gardens. They're said to be highly intelligent, and they have this recommendation, that they don't come creeping about our bedrooms and under chairs, and so forth.'

An archangel ecstatically proclaiming the Millennium, and then finding that it clashed unpardonably with Henley and would have to be indefinitely postponed, could hardly have felt more crestfallen than Cornelius Appin at the reception of his wonderful achievement. Public opinion, however, was against him – in fact, had the general voice been consulted on the subject it is probable that a strong minority vote would have been in favour of including him in the strychnine diet.

Defective train arrangements and a nervous desire to see matters brought to a finish prevented an immediate dispersal of the party, but dinner that evening was not a social success. Sir Wilfrid had had rather a trying time with the stable cat and subsequently with the coachman. Agnes Resker ostentatiously limited her repast to a morsel of dry toast, which she bit as though it were a personal enemy; while Mavis Pellington maintained a vindictive silence throughout the meal. Lady Blemley kept up a flow of what she hoped was conversation, but her attention was fixed on the doorway. A plateful of carefully dosed fish scraps was in readiness on the sideboard, but sweets and savoury and dessert went their way, and no Tobermory appeared either in the dining-room or kitchen.

The sepulchral dinner was cheerful compared with the subsequent vigil in the smoking-room. Eating and drinking had at least supplied a distraction and cloak to the prevailing embarrassment. Bridge was out of the question in the general tension of nerves and tempers, and after Odo Finsberry had given a lugubrious rendering of 'Mélisande in the Wood' to a frigid audience, music was tacitly avoided. At eleven the servants went to bed, announcing that the small window in the pantry had been left open as usual for Tobermory's private use. The guests read steadily through the current batch of magazines, and fell back gradually on the 'Badminton Library' and bound volumes of *Punch*. Lady Blemley made periodic visits to the pantry, returning each time with an expression of listless depression which forestalled questioning.

At two o'clock Clovis broke the dominating silence.

'He won't turn up tonight. He's probably in the local newspaper office at the present moment, dictating the first instalment of his reminiscences. Lady What's-her-name's book won't be in it. It will be the event of the day.'

Having made this contribution to the general cheerfulness, Clovis went to bed. At long intervals the various members of the house-party followed his example.

The servants taking round the early tea made a uniform announcement in reply to a uniform question. Tobermory had not returned.

Breakfast was, if anything, a more unpleasant function than dinner had been, but before its conclusion the situation was relieved. Tobermory's corpse was brought in from the shrubbery, where a gardener had just discovered it. From the bites on his throat and the yellow fur which coated his claws it was evident that he had fallen in unequal combat with the big Tom from the Rectory.

By midday most of the guests had quitted the Towers, and after lunch Lady Blemley had sufficiently recovered her spirits to write an extremely nasty letter to the Rectory about the loss of her valuable pet.

Tobermory had been Appin's one successful pupil, and he was destined to have no successor. A few weeks later an elephant in the Dresden Zoological Garden, which had shown no previous signs of irritability, broke loose and killed an Englishman who had apparently been teasing it. The victim's name was variously reported in the papers as Oppin and Eppelin, but his front name was faithfully rendered Cornelius.

'If he was trying German irregular verbs on the poor beast,' said Clovis, 'he deserved all he got.'

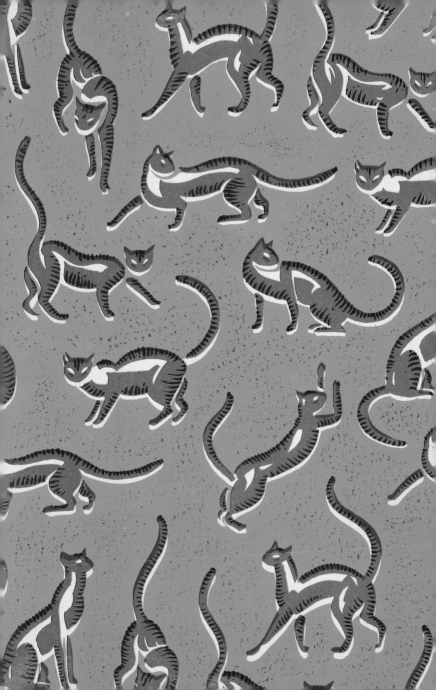